N E LINCS LIBRARIES
5 4073 02011468 4
D0537776

THIS BOOK BELONGS TO:

PAW PATROL™: PUP-FU POWER
A CENTUM BOOK 9781912707119
Published in Great Britain by Centum Books Ltd
This edition published 2018
1 3 5 7 9 10 8 6 4 2

Centum Books Ltd, 20 Devon Square, Newton Abbot, Devon TQ12 2HR, UK
books@centumbooksltd.co.uk
CENTUM BOOKS Limited Reg. No. 07641486

A CIP catalogue record for this book is available from the British Library

Printed in Italy

Pup-Fu Power

It was a special day for Farmer Yumi's martial arts students. The PAW Patrol, Mayor Goodway and Chickaletta were all gathered in Farmer Yumi's barn, eager to earn their Pup-Fu yellow belts.

"Students, are you ready?" asked Farmer Yumi. The pups quickly lined up and then bowed to their sensei.

One by one, the pups showed off their moves. Rocky twirled a staff and Marshall spun around.

Skye kicked high and Rubble stood tall. Zuma was ready for action.

Then Chase announced, "And now I will—

ah ... ah ... CHOO!

I'm sorry. I'm allergic to ... *kittens*?"

The Kitty Catastrophe Crew from Foggy Bottom had sneaked into Farmer Yumi's barn!

Mayor Humdinger had brought his team of mischievous kittens to prove that Cat-Jitsu was better than Pup-Fu.

"Pup-Fu rules! Cat-Jitsu drools!" Mayor Goodway said, folding her arms. "And there's nothing like Hen-Kido!"

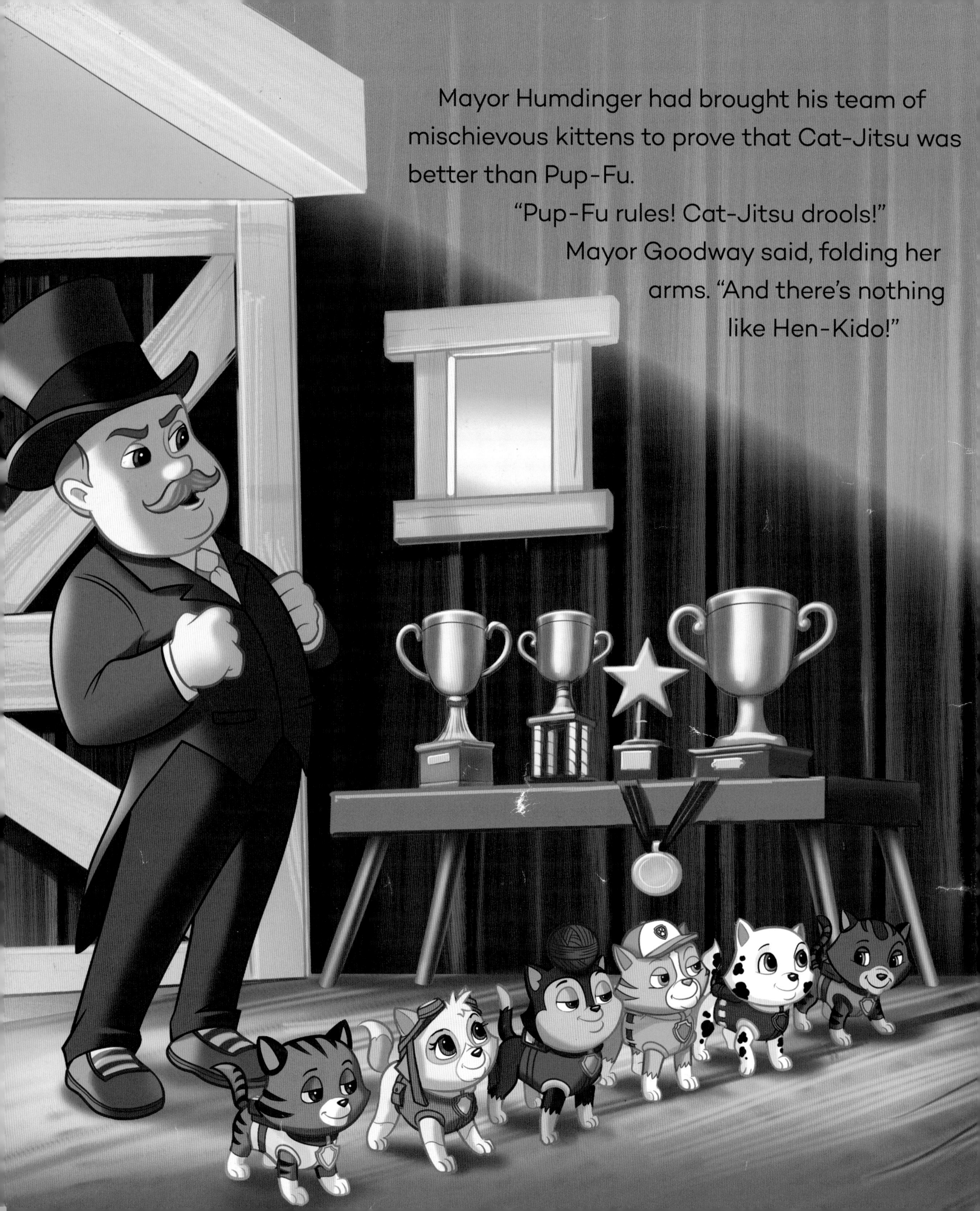

"*Bwok!*" Chickaletta clucked in agreement and gave a quick kick.

"It's not about which art is superior," Farmer Yumi said. "The point is for all pups, kittens, mayors and chickens to do their best."

Mayor Humdinger clapped his hands and his Kitty Catastrophe Crew sprang into action. They jumped and kicked and rolled on balls of wool. One kitten headed for the zip line.

"I'll show you how a Pup-Fu master uses the zip line," Marshall said as he jumped up and grabbed the cord. "Wheeee!"

The mischievous kitten hooked a mechanical claw onto the line and gave it a good shake.

Ziiing! Marshall went flying!

Marshall crashed to the ground.

"Are you okay?" Rubble asked.

"Yeah," Marshall replied. "Pup-Fu masters always know exactly how to land when they fall."

"For the next part of our belt test, we'll have sparring," Farmer Yumi said.

The pups and kittens began to spar. Marshall and a kitten in blue bowed and then sprang into action. Marshall jumped and spun through the air.

The kitten launched a ball of wool from her pack.

“Whoa!” Marshall yelped as he fell to the floor. His legs were wrapped in wool.

“Pup-Fu?” Mayor Humdinger snickered. “That looks like pup fail!”

It was time to award the belts. Farmer Yumi gave each pup a golden yellow belt. She was proud of them and their dedication to Pup-Fu. "Your extra-hard work would please the ancient masters."

But there were no belts for the kittens.

"Mayor Humdinger," Farmer Yumi said, "until your kittens learn to control themselves and their tools, I'm afraid they cannot earn their yellow belts."

"Hooray for the PAW Patrol!" Ryder cheered. They were all good pups – and they were all very good sports.

The End

PUP-FU POWER QUIZ TIME

1. What is the pups' martial art called?

2. What colour of belt do they all hope to earn?

3. What kind of animals are in The Kitty Catastrophe Crew?

4. Which pup gets his legs tangled in wool?

LET'S SEE WHAT YOU REMEMBER FROM THE STORY. ARE YOU RUFF-RUFF READY?

LET'S ROLL!

Answers: 1. Pup-Fu, **2.** Yellow, **3.** Kittens, **4.** Marshall.